I WANT A SAINT BERNARD

BY RHIANNON DRAKE

Ebook ISBN: 978-1-964451-89-3
Paperback ISBN: 978-1-964451-90-9
Hardback ISBN : 978-1-964451-91-6

I knew a little girl,
who was certain about what she wanted.
When other people (always grown-ups) tried to discourage
her, she was gracious but undeterred.

Once I asked, "Doesn't it bother you when they say 'No,
you don't want that' after you just said you did?" She replied,
"No, because I know what they mean. What they mean to say
is they wouldn't want it, and that is alright. It is okay to like
different things."

Even at a young age, this girl was willing to
assume positive intent in the people around her,
without giving up her personal beliefs.
I think about that moment quite often.
So often, in fact, that I wrote a book about it.

For Amyrissa,
who knows what she likes,
and has always respectfully stood her ground.

And for Boomer,
who is what Amyrissa likes.

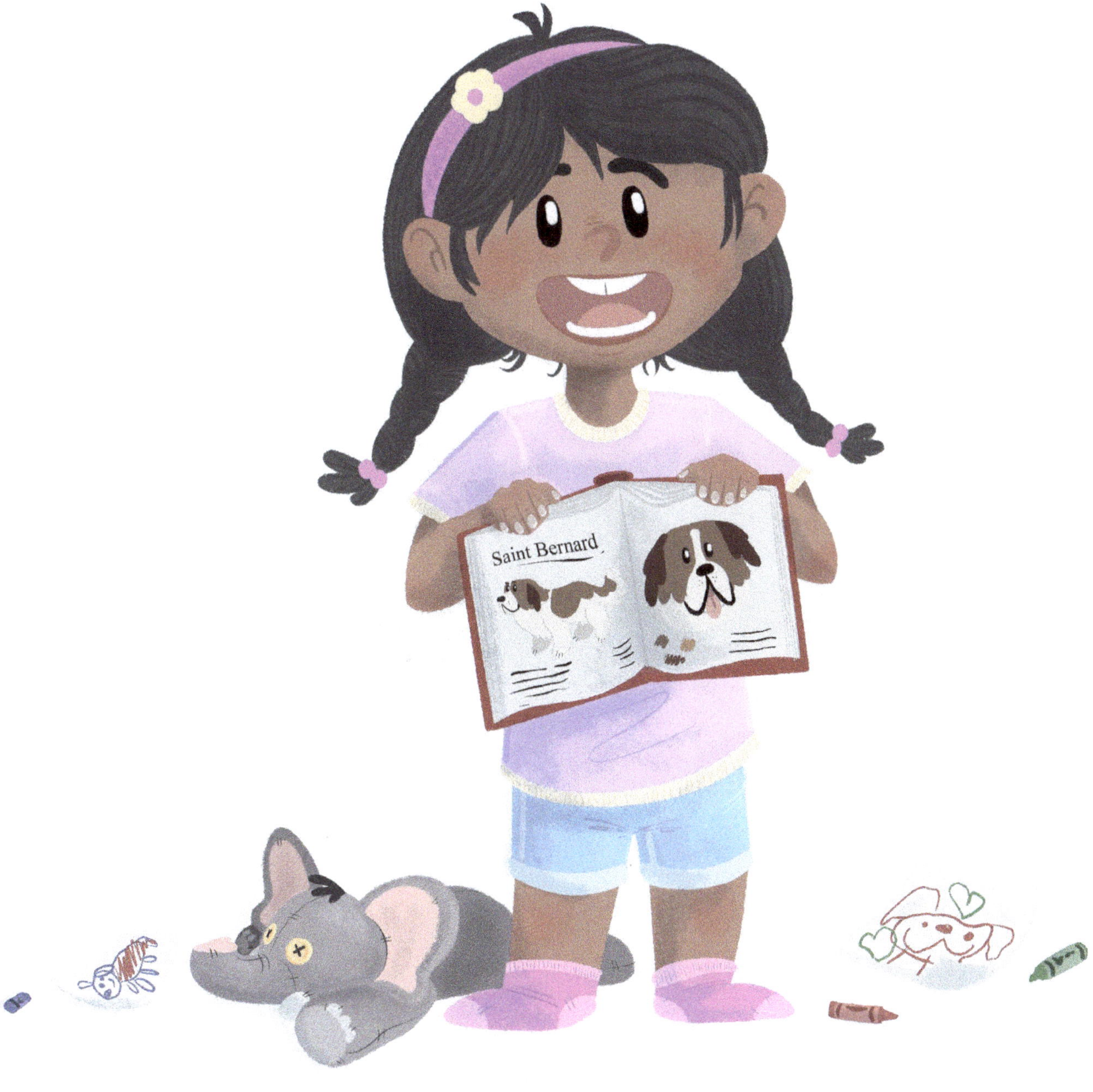
Saint Bernard

I want a Saint Bernard!

No

You

Don’t!

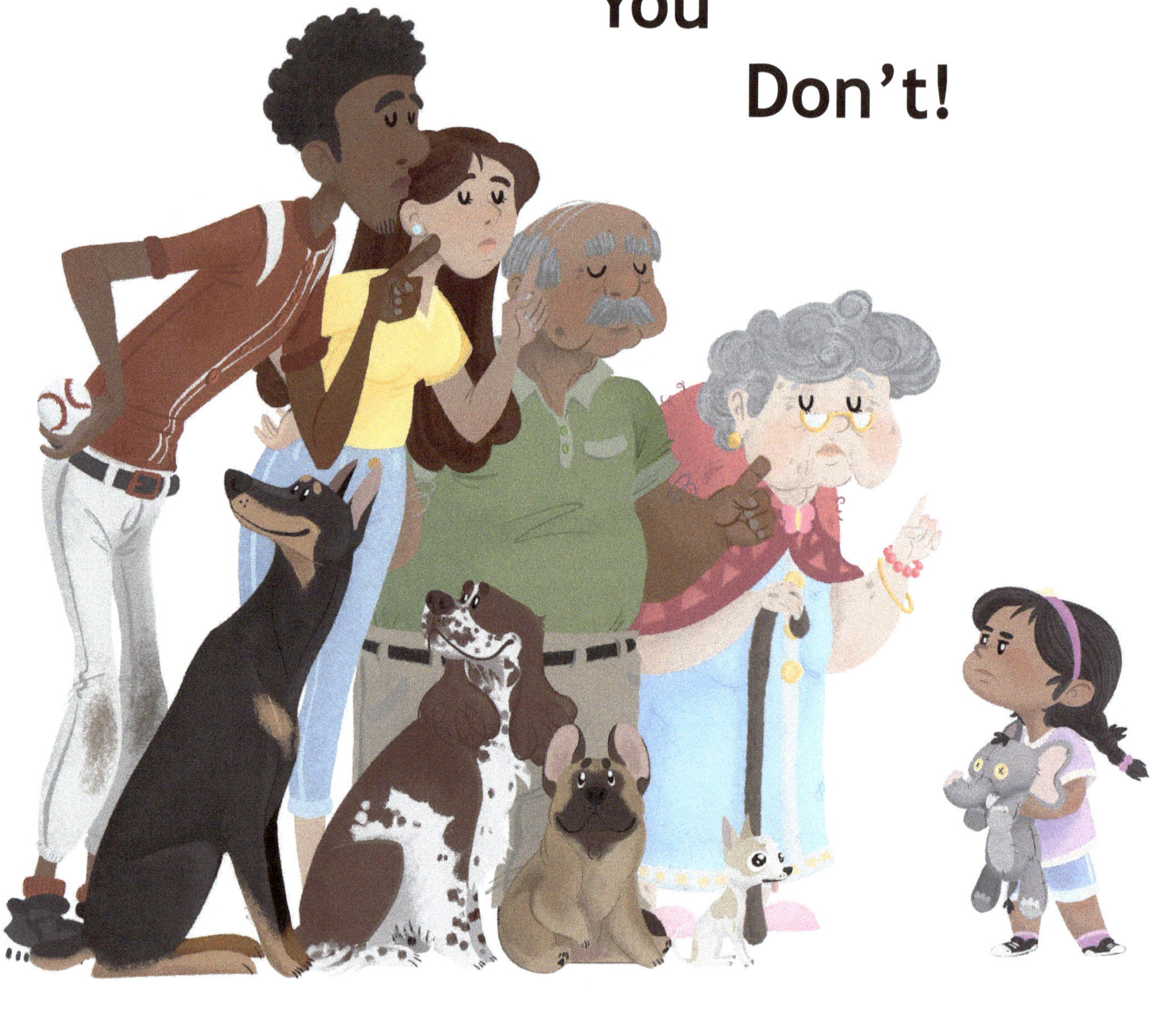

Yes,
I think I do.

I want to hug my Saint Bernard.

There will be way too much drool.

Everything will get soggy and gross.

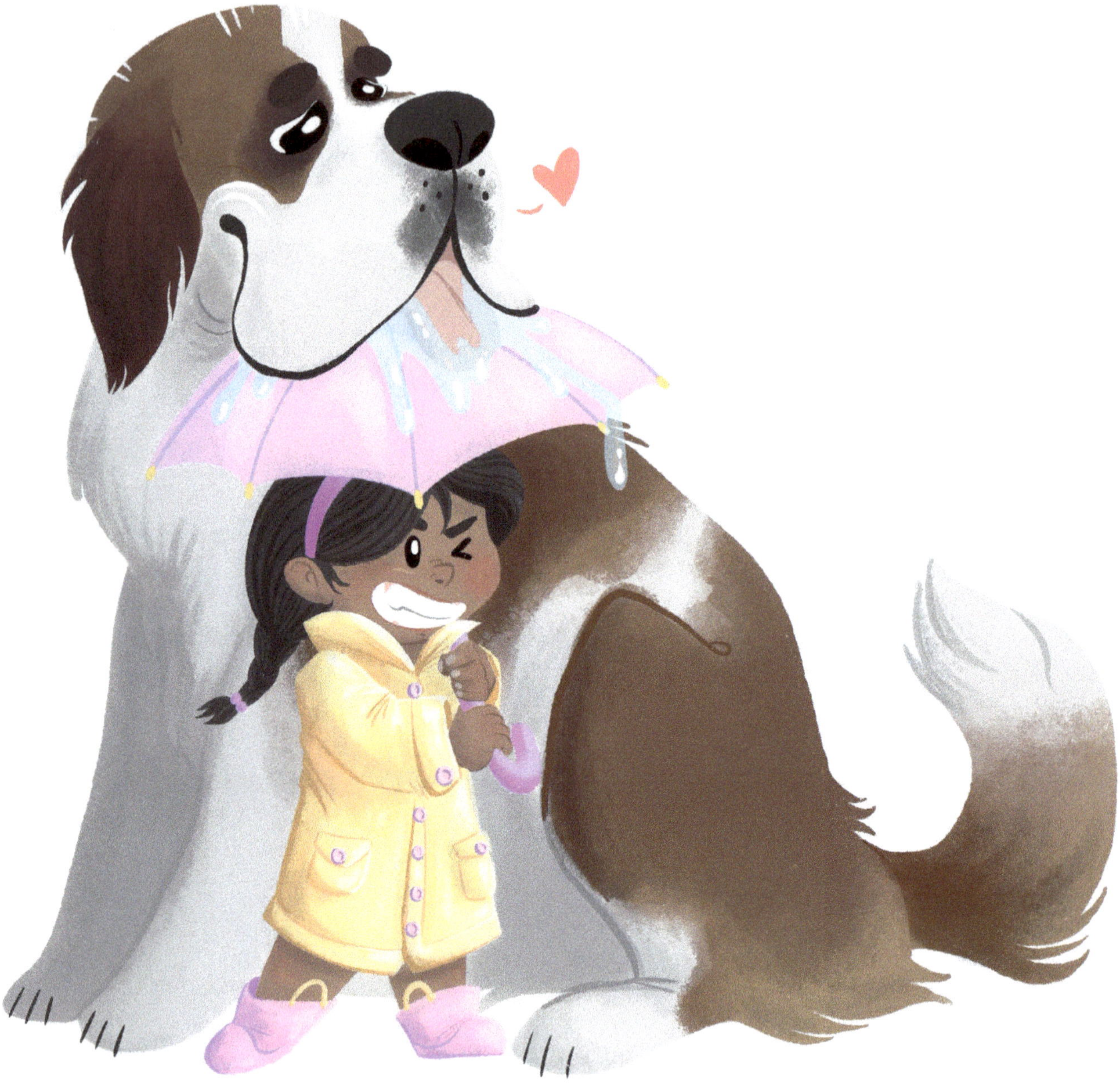

I do not mind.

I want a Saint Bernard.

I want to walk my Saint Bernard.

That dog is too big for you.

It would pull you down.

That will not be a problem for me.

I want a Saint Bernard!

I want to groom my Saint Bernard.

That is a mountain of hair.
You will say "It is too much work."

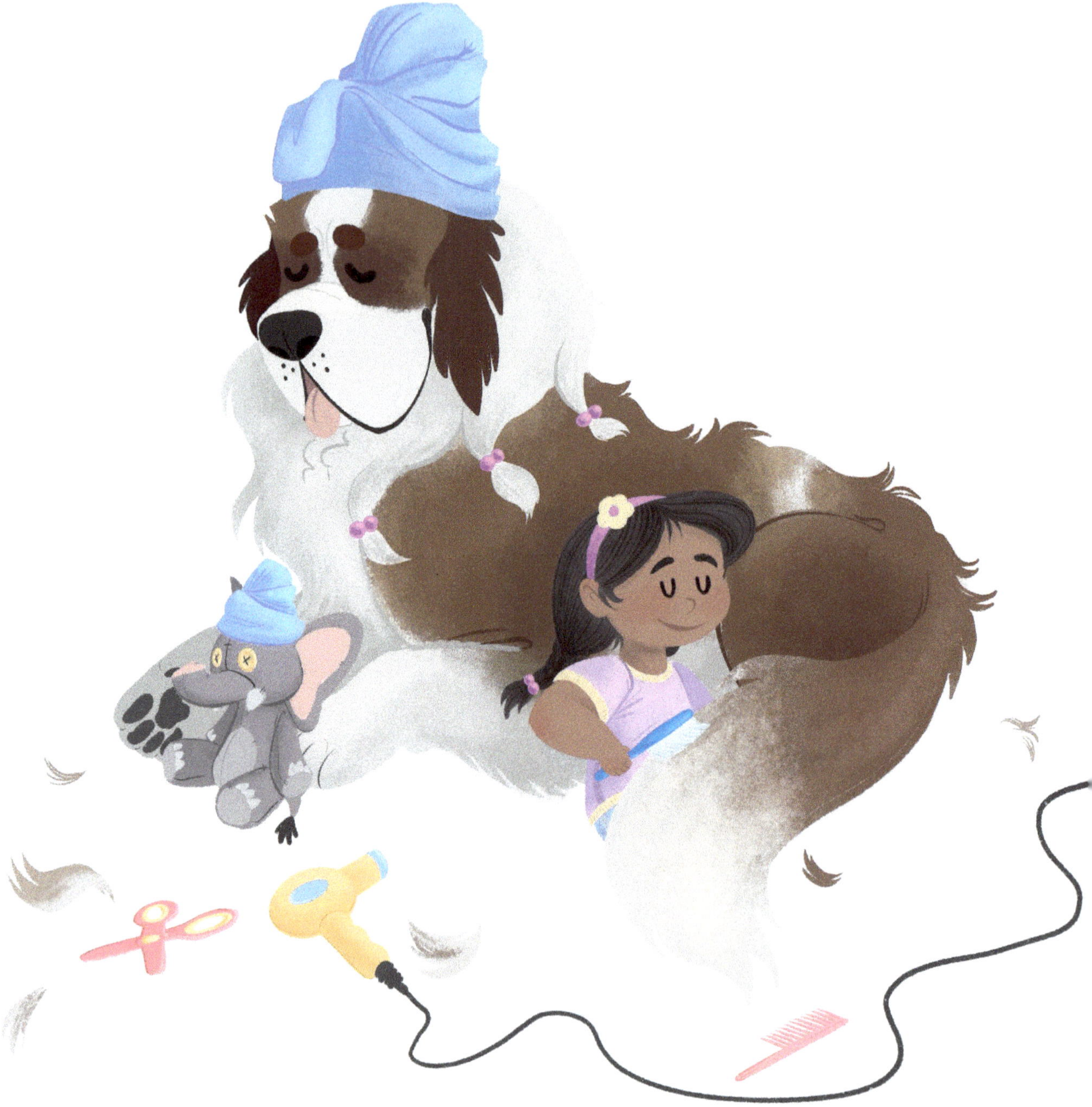

I do not feel that way.

I want a Saint Bernard!

I want to play with my Saint Bernard.

Such a big dog will knock everyone over. You will not have any fun.

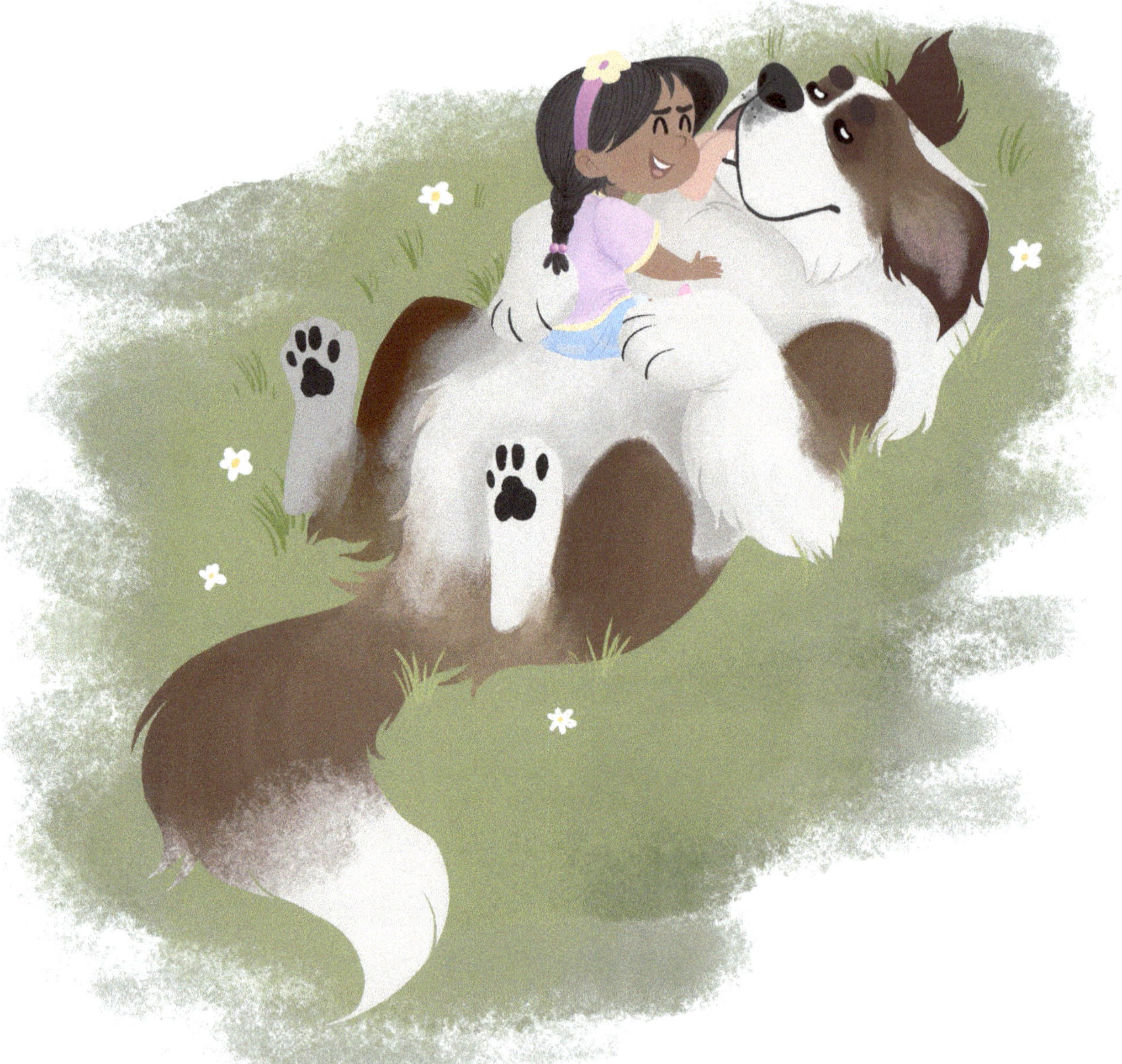

That is not how I see it.

I want a Saint Bernard!

I really want a Saint Bernard!

The only thing that could
be better than a
Saint Bernard

Would be two Saint Bernards!

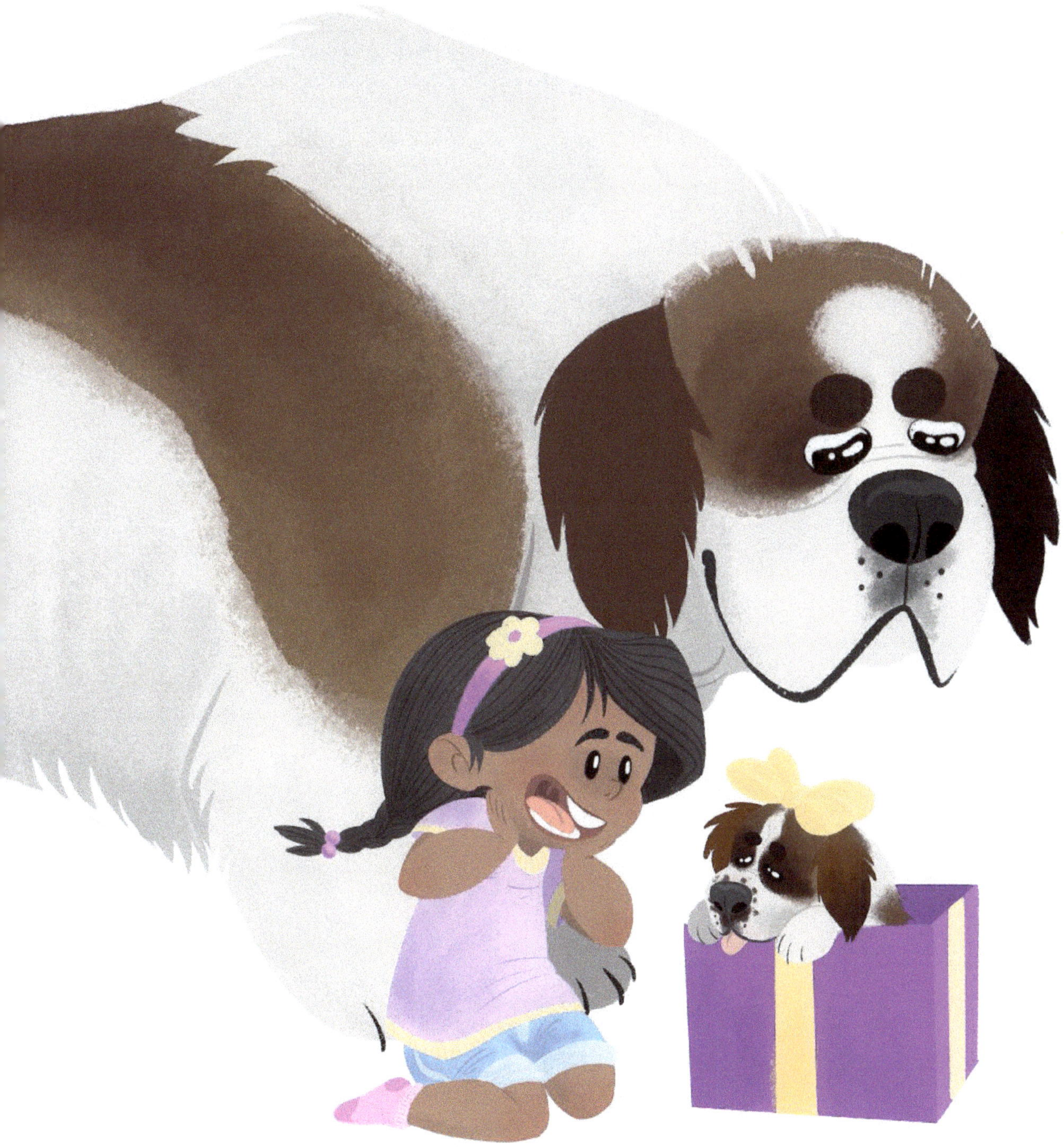

The

End

Famous St. Bernards

Barry

Considered to be the most famous St. Bernard dog, Barry worked at the Hospice of St. Bernard between 1800 and 1814. He is reported to have saved more than 40 people from the Swiss Alps' icy conditions. To this day, those who visit the Natural History Museum in Berne, Switzerland, can see an exhibit dedicated to Barry.

Beethoven

the star (and namesake) of a series of much-loved movies rose to fame in 1992, when his first movie earned a spot on several lists of all-time best dog movies. The sequel, "Beethoven's 2nd", was also popular. The two big-screen hits were followed by several made-for-video features.

Buck

St Bernard and Scotch Shepherd mix, Buck is the main protagonist of Jack London's 1903 short adventure novel The Call of the Wild. Buck is a pampered dog living in California before he is captured and sold. He is forced to work as a sled dog in the harsh conditions of the Yukon. When a man named John Thornton rescues him Buck begins to become part of the wild.

That's a fact

Who are you?

The Saint Bernard is a breed of very large working dog from the Western Alps in Italy and Switzerland. It might be cool to be born on a mountain!

Dogs at work.

Rescue dogs can smell a person buried under 20 feet of snow. And once they have found someone trapped under a snow heap, they use their huge paws to dig them out. So helpful!

Big Babies.

Saint Bernard puppies are tiny

creatures that weigh just 1½ pounds at birth. Adult dogs can weigh as much as 180 pounds. Because they get so big, they grow very quickly!

www.ingramcontent.com/pod-product-compliance
Lightning Source LLC
Chambersburg PA
CBHW041527120626
46551CB00018B/2606